Provolone

A short work

by

Ibrahim Diallo

A full copy of this book is available at idiallo.com

Publisher: Arab Idiom Hill
ISBN: 978-1-7368799-0-0

Table of Contents

You only see them in pictures or in the background, but they made me who I am. My wife, my mother, and my sisters.

To the women who defined me.

CHAPTER 1

Brooding

"Memory is a reflection of time. Only it is forged by desire."

It was mid-December. The sky was covered with some thick dark clouds and there was a chill. No wind, only a chill. Cold and still. The moment I see those clouds my shoulders sink. It doesn't matter how I'm feeling before I see them, even if I'm already in a dark mood. My shoulders always manage to sink a noticeable inch or two. My natural reaction to this weather is depression.

I was particularly feeling down on that day. Something bad might have happened, or I might have had a promotion at work. I can't tell. All I know is that the beautiful sun that usually appears at noon in my cubicle was nowhere to be seen.

I was on the twenty first floor of a reflective sky scraper. I had started on the third floor. I still remember what I wore on my first day. It was a plain white shirt, two sizes too big. Black pants that failed to express any fashion statement, and what looked like a noose for a tie. Growing up we used to call these clothes, “Thank you uncle.”

I never pictured myself wearing this at a job or anywhere else, but I had to look the part. My only inspiration for this abomination of style was, as you might have guessed, my uncle. He was one of those cool uncles all the children loved. He was the youngest on my father's side and a delight to talk to. We took him for one of us. And to add to it, he was only half an inch taller than me. So every time he parted with his old clothes I was first in the short line of inheritance. “Thank you uncle,” I would say. I'd try them on in my room then hear, “Is that a thank-you-uncle?” My brothers would ask.

My wardrobe has improved over the years but along the way I have developed a new mindset when it comes to what I wear. I have been accused of being ungrateful when I receive new clothing as gifts. I have nothing against a new pair of shoes mind you, especially when they fit so well and are lined for comfort. But what I find irritating is having to think about them. A shoe's purpose is to fit, protect, and keep my feet ache free throughout the day. But a shoe that forces me to be constantly vigilant for fear of getting them dirty fails at it's most basic job. I would rather wear an old pair that I can accidentally walk in a puddle with and not worry too much.

Anyway, I came into the job market with the enthusiasm of a boy ready to change the world. I've graduated top in my field as a computer engineer. Companies fought to have me work for them, in what turned out to be unpaid labor. I hopped from job to job laboring and proving myself, until a huge company had decided to hire me with pay. I stopped hopping. I came in from the third floor with a grin plastered on my face.

I remember the first time I saw The Designer. This company's logo was a blue silhouette with curvy hips inside a revolving ellipse. It was referred to as the

Designer in the welcome kit. Our motto was "We design the future" and yes, It was exciting to work at the edge of technology.

Those were the good days. Every morning was like going to a friendly competition where contestants could hug and shake hands. I knew all my co-workers. We spent our lunch time together, we met after work, and we joked around in the office. We made fun of those figures that stood in the back of the elevator. You could have a conversation with anyone on the floor and everyone was always eager to join the talk.

I loved those days.

Every milestone was celebrated with a free lunch where the whole team, including some of those figures, invaded a restaurant. We would laugh, drink, eat, toast, like it was our last day on earth. Yet these events were so frequent that I found myself expecting them every other week or so.

This all changed when I was promoted up to the tenth floor. It was like when you graduate from middle school and don't find your friends sitting next to you anymore. Now each class had a different teacher and next to you was a stranger's face.

Oh, high school was so cruel. I still wonder how the scrawny child that I was had survived those years. Some of my classmates had thick beards and large construction workers arms like they were part of the crew rebuilding the school's auditorium. I was the perfect candidate for bullying.

I had to be vigilant. For the better part of the years, I pretended I was from the student exchange program, adding a thick paste of India on my accent so they would think I did not understand their threats. It gave me a sort of diplomatic immunity and they quickly moved on to harass the next well-spoken kid. Tanweer, the Indian boy from the student exchange program, often looked at me suspiciously.

Anyway, work became like high school. Except here the cruelty was your coworkers trying to cheat you out of a promotion. The hardest was when some would pretend to be your friends just to stab you in the back.

Among a thousand, I would remember this one. Not his name, it's been so long, but it did rhyme with mine. He seemed so nice and eager to learn. He nodded for each instruction I gave. Each nod deeper than the one before, until the last one that turned into a sweeping bow. I would always end with a hand on his shoulder, like a friendly king saying “Rise! Worthy knight.” He would run to his desk, and follow my instructions to the letter. I was happy to have found at least one person who wasn't playing this game of deceit. An apprentice. A friend. But I was wrong. He was in for the throne.

Little did I know he was not new at all. He was playing the part to take credit for my work. I had willingly let him use my computer once. He made sure to access it every evening, signing all my work with his own name. Every morning, I would rename the files back, thinking it was a bug in the software that overwrote my name. Tired of the repetitive task, I wrote a script that renamed my work back to its original state every day. It silently worked in the background and I forgot all about it.

When it came for a promotion he became distant. When I passed him in the hallways he would pretend not to see me, or he would manipulate his phone with an urgent look on his face.

I received that promotion. I walked to his desk with a box carrying my personal belongings, hoping to give him last wisdom. He hissed when I called his name.

Then he presented me with his clutched hand and slowly unbowed his middle finger.

For each floor I climbed after, there was a similar scenario. Sometimes with two or three different actors. I felt gravity jealously holding me down. Technically, the grip of gravity gets looser as you climb at a higher altitude, but what the physics books don't tell you, is of the mental property you have to leave behind for every thrust ahead.

By the time I reached the twenty first floor, gravity had turned into shackles around my arms and ankles. My hair had started to turn white. My mental fuel was depleted. Getting up from bed had become a challenge. Work became the soul sucking void that was so close to draining the last ounces of life I had left.

But this job was all I was good at. It was all I ever did. I spent more time sitting in that cubicle than I spent anywhere else in my day. I was exhausted from the fight that it was to climb another floor, yet it was all I knew.

"You have climbed the corporate ladder faster than anyone I have ever met here." That's what the gray haired man in boxy suit told me for each promotion I got in the past five years. I always got promotions, but each made me sadder than the last. In doing my job right, I paid the price of leaving my close friends behind and made enemies. I will call them enemies because it was a fight to be in their presence. Defeating my enemies would have felt like a victory if only I couldn't see their wrought faces after.

On the eighteenth floor, I felt hope again. I thought I had found something. Something that would shatter my shackles and propel me into a better future. Someone, to be clear. I was happy for a moment. I had a romantic encounter.

It was this girl. I'm having a hard time remembering her face or her name, but oh, how beautiful she was. We always took the elevator to the same floor. It was so packed that we always ended up being carried away by the stream of people in opposite directions. All we could do was share a glance before she disappeared on the east side of the building and I on the west.

The day after another promotion, I found myself standing by the elevator. I turned left and right, there was no one. I stood in silence waiting for that slow, rumbling car that took an eternity to come down from the heavens. I looked left, I looked right, and there she was standing. No one else, just the two of us.

Oh how beautiful she had looked in her... Ah memory, so unfaithful. But I clearly remember the feeling of beauty.

When the door opened, she went in first, I followed. She pressed the buttons before I could. The door closed. We stood side by side. She must have made a sound. Something like a giggle. The elevator door was of a reflective gold, and I could see her... The lack of oxygen can play serious tricks on the mind.
Oh whatever.

I could see her beautiful eyes shying away. Through the reflection, she smiled a pretty smile with pearl white teeth. Her hair was a cascade of brown curls that turned into a tamed fire under the golden elevator light. She let go of her crossed arms and they came so close to mine. If only I had been standing closer. I made a silent prayer for a scenario where our hands brush slightly.

Saint Otis, of the order of Elevators answered my prayer in a heartbeat. The elevator jerked, slightly swinging her my way, like a brother looking out for me. I let myself swing in the opposite direction and pushed some more until our hands brushed. She turned and her eyes met mine.

It was like the first kiss under a tree, with grass dancing across the hills.

Ah that moment should have lasted forever. But it didn't. Instead, she swung away...

Another heartbeat later, her hand came back. Her fingers slipped into mine. Her skin was a milky brown and felt like silk. She spoke.

I had rehearsed this moment a thousand times. At night I would bring these images to my mind. Images where we were alone in the elevator and we would have long fruitful conversations. Conversations that led us to realize that we were made for one another and fall in love. But the real world is always so different.

Ding! The elevator door opened. We stood still.

I looked deep into her eyes. In that single look and our fingers tangled, I saw her entire story unfold before me.

She was God's answer to a thousand year old prayer. The perfection embodied in delicate hands, soft skin, beautiful lips, and glaring eyes. A woman with the strength to stand by you for the good and the bad. Here I was, lucky to be standing in the right place, at the wrong time.

She stepped out, her hand still in mine. I didn't move until she felt my grip. Today, I wasn't going to the west side. I was going one floor up, to the nineteenth. It was her stop. Not mine. She turned back, looked at my hand, then my eyes, her silk fingers slipped away. The door started closing almost too quickly. I caught a last glimpse of her. Her last expression. I croaked. All I saw was a frown that turned into my own reflection as the door closed shut.

Everyone always had the same expression when they were left behind. This was three floors ago. There were fifty floors in this building. What else will I lose before I get to the top?

CHAPTER 2

Jacket

“Lunch, let's go.”

He did not ask. It was a command. To tell you the truth, I'm not sure I knew who he was. I was in my cubicle with the tall glass window looking out a gloomy city, my jacket rolled and used as cushion for my lower back, my shoulders perched as low as they physically could when he interrupted my brooding. I turned off my computer screen, as suggested by that green initiative email, and followed him.

His face was plain. There was nothing remarkable about it. I followed him six steps behind in the long alley between rows of cubicles. His reflection rippled on the tiled marble floor as he disappeared left and right behind the little walls.

I stopped and waited for him as he made the rounds. I stood by to a cubicle. It was a red cubicle. It was the same size as mine but this one must have been decorated by Santa himself. It had garlands swirling between the walls in the most vivid colors. A little Christmas tree stood on the desk with light sparkling in intervals. Pictures hanged on the walls, a train track went in a loop between the screens, the computer, the tree, and the coffee mug. Add a fireplace and we would call it a family home. All I could think of was how hard it would be to pack all this in a box.

I failed to see the person sitting in the middle of this living-room. A short pinched face person looking back at me with a tea cup in hand.

"Oh! hey B!" said the little person in a high pitched voice. I did not know that this cubicle had existed a moment ago, so I did not know the occupant. I mumbled a response as the plain-faced commander came back with two more co-workers.

"Hey Brian", said one.

“Hey Bran”, said the other.

I nodded politely. The three, Santa's Little Helper, and I walked to the elevator.

What are their names?

In a fifty story building, there are many elevators. On our side, there were three cars that took their sweet time. On top of each door there was a panel with a number lighting up for each floor. I watched one of the panel as it went past forty-seven, forty-eight, forty-nine, and there was a long pause. I have never been past the forty-ninth floor.

All I know is that before a promotion, you get an email from “Management Group” with no reply address. You are instructed to calmly make your way to the forty-ninth floor and present yourself to “Becky” the receptionist.

“We've been expecting you Mr. Beric”, she always knew your name.

Becky would then lead you to a small room with a mirror wall where I counted an average of two hours wait time. Two hours in a room slightly bigger than a closet, watching your own reflection looking back at you. It's in this room that I've noticed my first strand of white hair. When you are about to reach enlightenment, a man in a boxy gray suit and gray matching hair comes to greet you. I met the same person for every promotion I got, and they were plenty. But this man was meeting me for the first time every single time.

He always started with a violent handshake which always took me by surprise.

“We are so happy to have you here. You are a valuable member of this company. Your work speaks for itself. In that spirit, we are going to give you a promotion”

He never asked questions that would lead to a conversation. I bet the only thing he knows about me is whatever was summarized in the thin manila folder he was holding in his hand.

When you get back to your desk, you would see a box with all your stuff neatly packed. A sticker will state where your new desk is, one floor up, and it is signed with a smiley face. I wonder if you would get the same treatment if you were getting fired, only the sticker would have a frowny face.

Ding! The door opened, and I followed these four strangers into a crowded elevator. The theme of the day was gray. Everyone was dressed in gray. Except for our colorful badges. We went three floors down before the door opened. A girl entered. She was all in gray and wore no badge. “Hi” I heard my self say.
“Hi”, she repeated.
She was proper. Her hair tied back, in regulations with work friendly hair styles. Her skirt the right size in that same unremarkable gray. She disappeared in the rumbling silence of the elevator.

No one looked left or right. No thoughts to share, no joke too long for a short elevator ride, no boring weather talk, no elevator talk. Nothing. Just the rumbling silence.

I was no different. I stood still like the figures in the elevator. I closed my eyes. I closed them very hard to picture the void I was hearing. Behind the rumbling silence, there was one even deeper. One that turns off the thoughts in your head. In that void, time slowed to an eternity. And right in the middle of it, emotions appeared. All of them, floating as pure energy, devoid of all their meaning. They hovered around me like prayers waiting to be fulfilled.

Suddenly I heard a giggle. I opened my eyes, looked left, looked right, there was nothing. No one moved or made a sound to own it. I dreamt it.

Ding! Everyone scattered like cockroaches. I followed my coworkers to the main exit. When the door opened, the wind rushed into the building disguised as a chill that made every hair on my body point North. "I forgot my jacket".

CHAPTER 3

Songs

Cars drove both ways on the street ahead, each creating a turbulent wind that sneaked into my clothes extinguishing any sign of warmth. Except for my feet. My new shoes were lined with thick cushy material that retained heat in.

“Thank you uncle.”

We were headed across the street for lunch. It wasn't much of a building but it looked authentic. There were people coming out of it laughing as if they had entered as workers and exited as friends.

It had unkempt brick walls, green vines grew between the crevices. If I ignored the surrounding buildings, this looked like a scene in a rural town in Tuscany. A little stone house in the countryside that stood the test of time. A river would pass through a spinning mill and the green grass blanketing the hills and dancing in a gentle breeze. The sight was enough to bring some warmth down to my spine. How did I not see this little village shack after all these years?

The door creaked and we were inside. My four companions did not seem to mind me at all. They headed straight to the counter where they discussed the menu. I stood in awe at the door. I was not only amazed at the fact that I had never seen this place before, but what intrigued me most were the people I came with.

I did not know who they were before, but they had the familiarity of old friends. I studied each of them. The one I called plain face spoke with his hands. For every word he said he had a hand gesture to go with it, like a manager breaking down a task for his team. One that I didn't bother to classify was a tall bearded man with dark glasses that were starting to turn transparent. The other had his sleeves pulled back revealing hairy arms. He looked more like a manual laborer than an office worker. Last was the pinched faced little person who was actually a girl. Santa's little helper is a woman. The things you don't notice.

“How is it going guys?” a voice greeted us from the kitchen. It was the room in the back of the deli where all the meals came from. It was hard to see anything inside. All I could think about is that it was not in regulation with a restaurant's kitchen. Food has to be prepared where the customer has full view of what is happening. I imagine those laws were put in place to prevent an angry cook from spitting in your food. But then I thought: I've never seen the kitchens of the restaurants we used to go to to celebrate milestones. Did I make up these laws?

Anyway. The words rolled out of my companions tongues. The menu was a musical sheet and they knew the song. The plain face lead the song with names I did not know then a symphony of ingredients. The others joined turning it into a quartet. The cook ended the notes with an approving kissing sound.

“Mmmuah, Good choice.”

Then it was my turn. They parted, each pair of eyes falling on me, waiting for my concluding solo.

“What about you buddy, what are you having today?” the cook asked.

The cook was a handsome man dressed in clothes too neat for a kitchen. He had a strong jawed face freshly shaven, gray green eyes and salt and peppered hair. His voice was like an arrow you shoot in the sky and it curves into an arc before it reaches it's target. The target was always comforted to receive it. The cook had a permanent smile on his face.

I wanted to answer but first I thought about my own facial features. If God had asked me how I would have wanted to look like on the molding table, I would've handed him a picture of this man. He did not look like a cook. He was tall, elegant. Under his apron, he wore a white buttoned-shirt and long black pants that ended with expensive looking shoes. He must had retired into a cook and was still used to wearing his office clothes. People who retired always found a new passion.

“You don't know what you want, do you?” He asked again. I was between thinking about my asymmetric facial features and trying to understand the menu. These were the words that were supposed to describe my next meal. I had no clue what they would translate to in food form.

My voice was a plummeting curve. The first word always comes out much higher than the next. The second is higher than the third. The third fades into a mumble that rendered my statements incomplete. I was not sure how things were supposed to sound like when they came out of my mouth.

"What kind of bread do you want?" He asked. "What do you recommend?" I answered with a question. He listed a thousand different kind from what I would call, the bread compendium.

"I'll have the first one."

"Ah, Good choice," he answered. "Now what kind of meat?"

Again, I looked at the menu handwritten with chalk on a long blackboard above. No it wasn't a musical sheet. Under meat there were so many things. I tried to read them in my mind.

Mortadella, Bologna, Lebanon, Pepperoni, Cotechino, Capicola, Soppressata, Pastrami, Bresaola, Ravioli, Guatemala, Finocchiona, Chorizo... I'm sure I made some of those up. Just like I had turned to an exaggerated Indian accent in high school, I decided to wear my Italian mustache. You just have to raise the tone on the syllable before last, stretch it and then gracefully descend into the last. It would make a beautiful solo.

But I did not know which was crocodile meat, and which was chicken. So I went for the clever answer: “As long as it's not pork,” that way he would have to make that decision for me.

“Oh, I know just what you are going to like. Now what kind of cheese? Do you want any cheese? You must have cheese.”

Why is it so hard. Cheese? I never add cheese. But he said I must have cheese. So I looked at the blackboard once more and under the cheese column it had words handwritten in cursive. I had to tilt my head and get closer to decipher what it was saying. I felt like I was climbing the counter at some point before I finally decided.

“Provolone is good.” Another voice beat me to it.

“Yes, that.” I replied. It wasn't the cook that answered. He was gone. Well, I took too long and since he was to make my companions sandwiches he had moved back into the kitchen. It was a short man wearing a hairnet and a food stained apron that answered. He rang my order but before I could reach for my wallet, the hairy arms handed him a credit card. He gave me two violent pats on the back.

“Don't worry Bran. First lunch is always on us.” he grinned.

“Thank you”, I said in the thickest Indian accent I had ever done. Far away, an Indian boy named Tanweer must have chocked.
I went to the nearest table where my companions were now seated. It was a small metallic table surrounded by four chairs each occupied by a bottom. They were all very nice people. I wanted to ask their names.

“Bring a chair over,” the beard said. His voice was surprisingly soft for a man of his stature. When I come back I will tell them I don't know their names. There is no shame in telling the truth.

I went to the table by the wall to grab a chair, but something else caught my attention. There were paintings on the walls. Old scenes from the times people did everything with their own hands. Farmers.

The whole family woke up at sun rise and headed for the fields. The men grabbed long scythes and scattered throughout the fields reaping what they sowed. The children were naked and played by the water, where an old rubber tire had been tied to a tree branch. A separate picture depicted the women.

They were in a barn, dressed in long brightly colored dresses. The young girls were laughing as they made large discs of cheese, while older women were further back milking a cow. I wondered if the painter had asked the girls to say “Cheese” before capturing the moment.

Then I turned to look at the deli. It was lit by the natural gloomy daylight coming in from a window, yet it was colorful. The lower part of the walls were decorated with carved wood in shape of wild flowers. The upper walls were a fabric wallpaper patterned with assorted vegetables. At that moment, I tried to remember my cubicle walls. I have no clue what color my cubicle walls are. I must have looked at the decoration for a while because when I finally joined the table with a wooden chair in my arms they were all standing. They each had their food in a bag and were waiting for me.

“I'm sorry, but I have to ask...” I started.

“Don't worry, we will wait for you. Then we can go eat by the park. That's where we eat lunch.” Santa's little helper said.

That's not what I was going to ask. These are strangers. I didn't even know their names? They were standing in a half circle, partly surrounding me and I had waited long enough without saying a word. I didn't speak. Instead, I thought.

Strangers are only one step away from becoming friends. The rules for friendship are not so complicated. You say a few words, you make each other laugh, then you are friends. Names can come later. What is a name but a label. I can tell salt from pepper just by looking at one of the shakers. I don't need to have the name painted on it.

“He must be milking the goat for my cheese.” I said. They chuckled.
I had done that before. In the lower floors, I have called people friends and they turned out to be the exact opposite. But maybe it is time I use a different approach.

From now on, these would be the people I would take the elevator with to go to lunch. Whether our relationship turn into something meaningful or go astray, I will cherish the little moments. Just like someone would cherish a deep conversation with a friend.

“You guys go ahead, I'll meet you there as soon as my food is ready”.

“It's the park right across the street. There are benches and tables under the tree. OK?” The plain face instructed and drew a tree in the air.

“OK. I'll be there”.

Such a deep conversation among friends.

The hairy arms gave me another pat in the back before they left. This time it was gentler.

They walked out playfully. Laughing, cheering. I returned my chair to the table and sat alone.

“It's almost done my friend.” The cook said, sticking his head out off the kitchen.

“No problem, take your time” I answered. I made friends.

CHAPTER 4

Puddle

I walked closer to the counter to see the inside of the kitchen. The closer I got, the better my eyes adjusted to the darkness. The cook stood in front of a large rectangular table in the center where all sorts of condiments were scattered in no particular order. His hands slid like a serpent, beating and twisting some dough until it turned into a bun. He was covered in flour up to his elbows where his sleeves were folded and he wore no gloves.

He must had done this motion a thousand times, yet he did not look like a cook. He looked like the man leading the conversation in a lively meeting. One of those rare people that could make an audience laugh in a tense situation, yet still say the important things that need to be said.

In the kitchen, he walked from corner to corner, sprinkling something here and there with a pinch of his fingers, tossing things in a pan, spinning a bottle in the air before letting only a few drops drip. And then tossing the tray of bread in a fiery oven that spat fire. I could almost hear the invisible crowd cheering while he performed his one man show. He was at ease.

Somehow with all this commotion in the kitchen, his shirt, his pants, his shoes were spotless. He could hang his apron, wash the flour off his arms and show up to work in our office. No one would even suspect.

On the forty-ninth, I saw people like him. Granted that I was only allowed to the small closeted room up there. But on the way to my promotions, I would steal a quick glance in the corridors. The floors were carpeted. They didn't suffer the white fluorescent light of the typical office. The whole floor was lit by golden natural light coming through the window and small dimmed spotlights. Here, tall handsome people that dressed elegantly, moved about like they were in the lobby of a hotel. It did not look much like an office building.

I have stopped trying to see what else was up there. I feared giving myself too much false hope. The twenty first had nearly destroyed me mentally. I have the white hair to prove it. I can't even imagine how I would feel going up more floors.

“Almost done buddy.” The cook said again with a smile. I smiled back and went to my seat. There was a second door in the back of the deli. This one looked more like a door you would see in a house. The top ended in an arc where triangles of fogged glass let in the day light.

I had nothing better to do then wait for my food, so I went to explore it. There was a standing shelf-like object next to the door blocking the way by an inch. It was covered with an unappealing brown sheet. When I used the tip of my shoe to nudge it aside, it squeaked and rolled away like it was standing on wheels.

I turned to see if anyone had noticed me but there was only one other customer in the deli and he did not seem to mind me at all. It was an old round man with hair coming out of every part of his body except where it mattered: his head. He was reading a newspaper and from time to time he would slap it with the back of his hand and mutter some obscure insult.

There were playful shouts coming from behind the door.

“How did this get here?” I heard a child's voice.

I turned the knob and pulled the door open and their voices came in with the chill.

“I saw it first. Don't touch it.” the older one yelled.

“It's mine. I'll tell dad. DAD!!!” The younger one screamed.

“OK Fine. You play with it first, then you let me” the girl said to the little boy.

“OK” the little boy agreed. But now that he didn't have to fight for it, he had no clue what to do with the toy. It was a big doll's head.

It was the size of a human head with synthetic brown hair and eyes painted directly on the skin. Blue skin. A shiny blue plastic head with synthetic brown hair. I had seen one of those back in college. To go to the engineering building, I had to pass through the fashion building. There, some tall girls with long legs, worthy of a magazine cover, were each carrying a mannequin's head just like this one. All the heads had the same hair do. I think it was a hair-styling class.

But this one was blue. Not very realistic.

The children were playing a dull game where it seemed they had not decided on the rules yet. They stood in the middle of the yard and passed the head to each other in turn. Behind them, this backyard lead to a vast garden where trees and flowers expanded beyond the little deli. The yard was covered in a tiled stone floor with gardening tools, woodwork, and a tool shed. Then it turned to a pebble path that lead into the garden.

Next to the tool shed there was a hose tied around a metal bar under which a small puddle had formed. The water was still as glass and perfectly mirrored the dark clouds.

The little boy saw me and held on tighter to his doll. “I'm telling dad you took the doll from me.” he threatened his sister one more time for no particular reason.

“What's all the noise? Who is calling me?” the cook asked. I moved over to the left to let him out in the backyard.

“It's nothing.” the little girl replied in a dull voice. “We were just playing.”

“Gaby didn't wanna share.” The little boy screamed. “I did share, you are holding her!” The girl protested. The boy looked down his arm where he was holding the doll, but had nothing to add.

“We're just bored”, Gaby added.

“Bored? In this day and age? You are bored? Come, let me show you what she can do.” The cook walked towards me. I made way again to let him back in. This time I stepped to the right, right into the puddle. It was deeper than it looked. The water splashed and my shoe drank it all through that thick lining that had kept my feet so warm.

“Not my new shoes!” I complained silently. The little boy giggled. “Don't talk to strangers,” the girl whispered.

“I didn't talk”, the boy replied in kind.

The cook pulled the brown cover off the concealed object by the door. Under it was the rest of the mannequin's body dressed in stylish clothes with untrimmed seams. It looked creepy.

He pushed the wheelchair over the sill of the door almost too delicately. As if he was pushing a real infirm person out of a hospital.

“Hand me her head Ari,” he asked his son.
Their father walked to the metal bar where the water hose was coiled. For a moment he struggled with the little red valve that refused to twist, it hissed like an angry cat before giving in. A weak stream of water dripped into the puddle breaking the reflection of the sky.

“I think she is thirsty.” The cook said, winking at the children. He lowered the mannequin's head and the water dripped in a small hole between its painted lips.

When the plastic head was filled, he inserted it onto the body and it snapped right in place. He wheeled the chair in the middle of the backyard and walked back to the children.

“Now watch. Tell me this is boring.” he said, kneeling beside them.

What could possibly happen? I was standing by the door, my arms crossed and under my armpit protecting them from the cold weather. My right foot wet, cold, and uncomfortable. I was both confused and excited for what was to come. Whatever it was going to be.

The sun appeared on queue from behind the clouds, bathing the mannequin into a warm light before disappearing once more. The mannequin seem to have absorbed the light as the pale blue turned eerie. And just like that the little wheels squeaked.

My eyes opened wide. The little boy clung onto his father. The little girl covered her mouth with both hands, to prevent a squeal from coming out.

Then the wheels squeaked some more and the wheelchair moved about. “Daddy Daddy, it's moving.” the little girl shouted excited. Her brother hid behind their father.

The wheelchair continued to move on its own towards the tool shed. Then it stopped. It rotated on itself making clicking sounds until it faced the opposite direction. Then it started rolling forward towards the little family.

My jaw dropped. If there was a bee in this garden, it could have settled in my mouth and raised a decent family. The little girl was excited and started skipping around the wheelchair and the stiff mannequin riding it. The little boy was curious, but still held on to his father's shirt for good measures.

“Go on Ari. Don't be afraid.” The father said, putting his hand on the armrest.

The boy let go of his father and touched the armrest. His eyes looked unsure as if the automaton was going to hurt him. But his sister grabbed both his hands and dragged him into a dance around the blue doll. Ari's fears melted away and he started laughing in a high pitch voice.

I closed my eyes, rubbed them, then opened. Repeated once more. Each time hoping it was a dream. What was happening?

I was not dreaming. But I had this weird taste in my mouth.

This was both amazing and creepy. I expected nothing, and this was more than I expected. My first explanation was a wind-up doll. But how could it be so big? It was a mannequin. The kind you would see posing in a clothing store, wearing the latest fashion threads to lure you in. A mannequin is not a toy. On top of that, what did water have to do with its movement? Then I stopped trying to understand.

The cook walked away slowly as the kids were screaming and playing. He walked to me and put his hand on my shoulder, let out a chuckle before he continued back into his kitchen.

My eyes never left the scene. It was like watching a dream leap into reality yet you were awake. I forgot that I was there to eat. Curiosity is surprisingly appetizing.

I watched the wheelchair roll, stop, turn and speed up. The mannequin was sitting on it, it's mouth slightly open and its eyes absent. It was going back and forth in the yard and the kids ran away from it. They pretended it was chasing them and they ran laughing.

Ah, laughter. What a pleasant thing.

CHAPTER 5

The Sandwich

I was still standing at the door, my arms crossed, my shoes soaked wet, the children laughing and running around, the mannequin whizzing and whirring.

Half way through the yard the mannequin came to an abrupt stop. That was the end of it. But it clicked and clacked as it turned on itself once more. This time facing the water hose, the giant doll wheeled itself to it.

The children ran around the yard, playing on their own. I focused on the mannequin.

It rolled on the puddle and stopped. It was close enough for me to look at every detail of its making. I never moved, only watched. It stayed still. Its absent eyes looking straight into the wall. It was dressed in a pale pink and silver dress with loose threads on the seams.

Suddenly, the mannequin's back bent mechanically until it was at the same level as the tip of the hose which was still dripping. The mannequin unnaturally turned its neck until the water slid through its mouth.

My jaw went as low as it physically could. The mannequin had gone to refill on water, all by itself. How in the world is that possible? Here I was, convinced that it was just a wind-up toy, but it was much more. I wanted to believe that it was a girl trapped in the body of a mannequin. Someone cast a spell on her or my hunger must have gotten the best of me.

But there were no reasons to believe that I had fallen asleep and into a dream. It was mid-day and the sky was covered with thick gray clouds that had turned the world into darkness. My natural reaction to this weather is depression.

But I was not depressed right now. Only confused. In the office, I am often presented with challenges no one knew how to solve. When I inquire what the problem is, they often resulted in a long rambling about how things never work, how someone else is stupid, and that we have incompetent engineers. I always want to ask them, “How does your rambling contribute to help solve the problem?”

Instead, I would break down the problem into little modules, separate the parts we know from those we don't. Catalog everything into small cards that I place on a whiteboard where everyone can see. Now, as a team, we work our way in one little problem at a time until we thoroughly solve it. Most often than not, the final solution appears before we complete the process.

So this was only a challenge. The mannequin performed complex movements, therefore it must have been powered by software, it was not just a mere automaton. The software drove some complex motors that also explained the clicking sounds when the wheelchair rotated. And those poorly painted eyes? Two infra-red cameras in disguise. Very effective in feeding data to the environment recognition software. That's all there was to it.

Oh, the water. The water performed two tasks. It circulated in the water cooling system, keeping the machinery at the optimal operating temperature. And, it doubled as a hydraulic pump for movement. Problem solved.

But all my explanation evaporated when I heard a gulp. The mannequin straightened back up, slowly curving its feminine spine. It looked too natural.

I made a step forward, splashing into the puddle once more. She turned and I saw her face. It was still blue, her hair the same synthetic brown. But her eyes. My God. The little wheels squeaked softly and suddenly she was in my face.

I felt somethings loosening in my bowels. Her eyes were not merely painted on the plastic skin as I thought. They were real. Her pupils dilated, her eyelashes fluttered, the white in her eyes moist.

Her skin was not so shiny anymore, it felt soft and fleshy. Her lips smacked. She clicked and clacked toward the children once more. Our eyes met for an instance, but I turned away immediately. She continued towards the children. I could have sworn, that smirk was not on her face before.

A hand landed on my shoulder and startled me.

“Hey buddy. Here's your sandwich.” It was the cook.

“Sandwich?” I said as I turned to him confused. “Oh yes, the sandwich”, I remembered and grabbed the warm sandwich that was wrapped in white paper. I was not hungry. Instead, I wanted him to explain what I had just witnessed. I wanted to ask him. He was looking straight ahead. Not at me but past my shoulder and he was still wearing a smile, but his eyes were serious.

“My son,” he said to me. “I tried to read him stories at night when he was younger. He didn't like it. He used to say, 'I don't believe you daddy.' What do kids know about believing? They're supposed to accept everything that comes from their parents, right? But not my Ari. So one day, I asked him. 'Why don't you believe the story? It's the same story mom used to read to you.' You know what he said? He says because I have no imagination.” He laughed. I chuckled.

“Eat your sandwich, it's better when it is warm.” The cook said. I was supposed to join my new friends at the park where we would eat together. They were probably waiting for me. But I didn't want to offend the cook. And who knows what he would do to my meal in that obscure kitchen next time if I refused. So I peeled off the wrapping and took the first bite.

That taste.

"Run! Run! She's gonna catch you!" the children screamed and laughed. The doll whirred behind them. So, the cook continued.
"My wife. She was a good mother. Sometimes when I come home at night, I would find them all in the bedroom. She would be in the middle surrounded by all the children, reading from a thick book with no pictures. The kids loved it, for them it was like watching a movie with special effects and the characters were alive and wore costumes. At least that's how it felt for me. I'm a big kid, what can I say?

"I wouldn't want her to stop, so I would just stand outside the bedroom and listen. Sometimes I'd be there for thirty minutes, my briefcase still in my hand, just listening to her making different voices for each character. Sometimes I would laugh and they would catch me. They were always so happy to see me. She was amazing. But I was an idiot.

“How do you like the sandwich” he asked. “I knew you are a particular eater, so I made something special.” I had a mouthful, so I chewed first, then chewed some more. I wasn't done chewing and savoring so I covered my mouth and answered.

“Oh, it's fantastic.” I had no clue what it was, but each bite was an explosion of flavors in my mouth. Every time I sank my teeth in the soft bread, I felt his story come to life. Some rich flavors danced in my mouth, spices tingled on one side, a faint sauce would wash it over, and when I swallowed, it was an orchestra. The meat was thin, red, and folded several times on itself. Some condiments, foreign to me, released a spicy aroma that rose through my nose and into my brain. The cheese was warm and pulled for every bite like it held the flavors together, then snapped. I slurped it into my mouth and it melted. I don't remember why I ever hesitated before, but by God, I love cheese.

“Yes, the sandwich is really good.” I repeated.

“I'm very glad.” he answered.

“Drink! Drink! Drink!” Ari was shouting behind us like he had never been shy or afraid before. No longer was he a wary boy. He was playing and running around, his voice a tad deeper then before. So, the cook continued.

“My wife, she was the real parent. She took care of the kids. She took care of me. She was a beautiful woman,” he said looking at the cloudy sky, squinting at an invisible sun. “But I was blind. I looked at her and I couldn't see her for who she was. I forgot that she was the woman I married. Instead, she became the woman that happened to be taking care of my children. I was out conquering the world, and I didn't have time for everyday non sense. You know how it is.”

I didn't know how it is. But I nodded all the same.

“Sometimes I used to spend all day in the office just to avoid her. I would come home very late, hoping that she would be asleep. But she would be up. Then she would ask me about my day like there was nothing. That would piss me off. So I would just say, 'yeah, fine' then end the conversation. I would go downstairs to my office and pretend I am doing something.

“She never complained. She looked more concerned than frustrated. Instead, I would hear her putting the kids to bed, then she would go to her little studio and work on her designs. The longer I stayed in that room, the more I realized how stupid I was. She had never done anything wrong. I felt, like life was too slow at home but that's not her fault. I was too proud to come out and apologize. But it's as if she could feel when I come back to my senses. She knew children, and she knew when they were done throwing a tantrum. At that time I would hear a knock on my door, and she would come in. She would smile, and I'd smile back. And everything was better.

"We forget. We forget how the important things come into our lives. So we break them, only then we remember how important they are. I have a hard time remembering her face when I close my eyes. I'm lucky that my daughter looks so much like her. I look at my wife's picture, but it doesn't show me what I remember." He pulled a picture out of his wallet and handed it to me. The juices were dripping from the sandwich into my hand. I had to guiltily wipe some of it on my pants before handling the picture. It was a beautiful picture. She had dimples and golden brown hair. She looked like a sweet woman anyone would be proud to call mom, or wife. She looked familiar, but not like the little girl playing behind me.

“You are right, she does look like your daughter” I lied. “Gaby? Is it?”

“Gaby? No, not Gaby”, he chuckled. “Gaby looks too much like me.”

Behind me I heard Gaby say, “She's sweet. I like her.” And Ari added, “And pretty. I really like her too.” So, the cook continued.

He leaned on the door, his eyes went down and then he sighed. “I killed her.”

The last bite I chewed caught in my throat.

“You know, they say if you yell negative words to a flower everyday, it will wither and die. That's what I did. The cancer that took her was probably all the bottled up anger that I had caused.

“Even when I knew she had cancer, it didn't stop me. It didn't make me better towards her. I was arrogant, and would even fight her about the cancer. Some times I would yell and argue about everything and nothing, the blood would boil in my body. She would join the fight and scream too. But then, she would stop. Not on purpose, I could still see the anger in her eyes. It was her lungs. She couldn't anymore. Here eyes would fill with tears, and she would whisper, 'Please'. Only then I would stop. It was like the evil spell cast upon me would break. I would open my eyes and see how much I had hurt her. I would embrace her in my arms full of regret. She never failed to embrace me back. She was dying.

“I don't think the children ever understood. At least not the little ones. All they saw was their mother losing weight. She had become so skinny. But the kids would keep asking her to tell stories. In the final weeks, I joined them during story time. I started sitting in and listening. I would sit on the lower end of the bed, my legs crossed and my hands carrying the weight of my head, like a little kid. That's when I finally understood what Ari was talking about when he said I had no imagination. You had to sit there to understand.

“You see, she wasn't just reading them a story. She was telling them one. The books were simple and boring. Everyone knows those stories. But when she read them, she turned them into a beautiful world a child can understand and relate to. She would change the story, she would add new characters on the fly. I started to like some of those new characters. It was so natural. My favorite was the king. She would say:

"'He lived in a castle as tall as the highest mountain. Over the years, he felt he had lost touch with the common folks he was ruling below. They would be afraid if the king came down suddenly to live among them. So every morning, he dressed as a kitchen boy and went down to the village to work among them.'

"I never asked her, but I felt this character was intended for me. But those were hard times. Everyday, a new part of her body was failing. Her skin became dry and pale, she couldn't retain water anymore. She was always thirsty, but no amount of water could quench her thirst. She was in pain. The children would beg her to tell another story, but she couldn't even open her mouth to answer.

"She became so weak she couldn't walk anymore. That's the wheelchair I got her." He pointed at it. The wheelchair was next to the puddle, still and empty. So, the cook continued.
"I tried to get rid of it so many times but every place I put it becomes the center of my life."

I had eaten half the sandwich and was trying to finish chewing this last bite before I could ask him a question. I asked anyway.

“So, how about the big blue doll?”

A speck of bread flew off my mouth and landed on his shoe. He paused. Little lights glinted in his eyes. He bent over, flicked the little speck off he shoes with a finger, and straightened back up.

“Ah, the designer. She was a designer. A clothing designer. When our second child was born, she took a break. She wanted to go back to work eventually but then she was pregnant again with Ari. So it turned into a hobby instead. She designed clothes just for friends and family. She used this mannequin for her designs. Every time I was grumpy, she would take it out and create something beautiful. That's how good she was. She would take my anger and mold it into something so beautiful that... She was perfect.” his voice broke.

“She is dead now.”

There was a long pause. I was afraid to chew or make any sound to disturb the one minute of silence. His eyes narrowed.

“They say, a loved one never dies under your watch. It's only when you dose off that they slip away. On that last day in the hospital, I sat next to her, held her hand and looked straight at her, never blinking, not even for a second. I wish I had never known that. All it did was make me see every last bit of it.

“My wife, she was suffering. She was in pain, whimpering. I didn't know what to do. I yelled, I cried for the doctors. She kept saying 'It hurts, it hurts so much.' I screamed for the nurses to come, never taking my eyes off of her, I didn't know what to do. They pushed me away from her side so they could help her. But I was still in the room, my eyes focused like lasers, never leaving her. Never blinking. I had to keep her alive.

“Then, I saw it. I saw that last moment where her soul tried to leap out of her body. It started as a long, slow, painful whimper, with her body tightening like stretched wood. I looked harder. She choked, her body twisted until I thought it would snap. The hair on her skin rose from head to toe, she squeezed the nurse's arm with un-feminine strength. I kept my eyes open, hoping it would keep her here, just a little longer. Her eyes and mouth opened so wide I thought they would tear apart. The scream came out of her mouth. I screamed and closed my eyes.

“It was only for a second, but it felt like an eternity being in the darkness. I saw her face. Oh what a beautiful woman she was. She had never stopped loving me. One heart beat later, I opened my eyes. She had stopped moving. But it was my wife laying there, with that same look in her eyes and a tear rolling down her cheek. I didn't want her to suffer any longer. So I let her go.” His voice broke.

“What do I tell the kids? What do I tell the family? What do I do? My wife, my best friend, the mother of my children, she is dead. I let her go.

“I don't know how I left the hospital. I appeared at my parents driveway to pick up the children. I never said a word. We drove home in silence. When I parked the car in the garage, I thought the little ones were sleeping. 'Where's mommy?' I heard my son ask. I wanted to tell him but I was crying. I cried. I cried like a child. I wailed like a widow. I couldn't take it. I just lost my best friend.

“I had closed my eyes to end her suffering, because I couldn't bare it any longer. But now it was my turn to suffer her absence for the rest of my life.”
We stood in silence together. His eyes were filled to the brim. I had nothing to offer but my ears. A moment later he pulled his apron up to wipe his eyes. So, the cook continued.

“My daughter, the eldest. She unbuckled her seat-belt and helped her brother and sister from their car seats. They all climbed to the passenger side where she held them in her arms and hummed a tune. She gave me her hand. I held it. She pulled me in to huddle with them. She had a smile on her face. That same beautiful smile my wife always wore. I stopped crying.

“'Do you know the story of the king that dressed as a kitchen boy?' she asked the children. Then she told the story. Ari and Gaby fell asleep in her arms. And I... listened. I listened.”

A single tear fell from his eyes. The smile was back on his face, he was happy. Though he looked like an old man now. He nodded and I understood he was done telling his story. He turned and walked back to the kitchen with long slow steps that echoed in the darkness as he faded away. I was left standing at the door sill.

There was silence in the yard. The children were gone. They left no laughter behind to fill the void.

CHAPTER 6

Forget-me-not

I took a few steps into the yard with half my sandwich still in hand. I headed towards the pebbled path that led into the garden. When I stepped on the first polished stone, I heard a loud thrum. I turned my head left then right, there was nothing. Nobody. Up in the sky, the building that housed my cubicle was so tall and lonely. The Designer had been swallowed by a thick gray fog.

I turned and walked back to the deli in complete silence. There was of course the squish and squash after every other step I took. It was as if my entire shoe was filled with water. I got to the door and saw that the deli was empty. In place of the old man was a neatly folded newspaper on the edge of the table. I was alone with the chairs, the tables, the counter, the paintings and the dark kitchen. Behind me, the door squeaked before it closed shut. Right then, I heard another loud thrum.

It shook me from the inside. It was one of those unusual sounds you don't hear with the ears. Instead it's a vibration that reverberates throughout your body. This place was no longer the joyful restaurant it once was. Now it was dark and the walls leaned in, like sinister giants that followed me with invisible eyes.

The cook was nowhere to be seen. I peeked into the kitchen but all I saw was a wall of darkness. Why did he tell me his story? I was a stranger to him and he had spent a good deal of time telling me a story reserved to close family members. I didn't know what to make of it. Was it supposed to be a lesson? I know that life only teaches you a lesson when you least expect it.

What is the lesson here? Was it about family? Children? Death?

It all started during my lunch break, but that must have ended a long time ago. He must have talked to me for hours because it was all dark now. My coworkers. My new friends. Could I still call them friends after abandoning them? They are probably back at work, talking behind my back, cursing me. They will never invite me to lunch again. But that's not what matters to me now.

I wanted to make a step forward to leave the deli but my feet were heavy. My shoes felt like buckets filled with water and refused to budge. I struggled helplessly.

There was not a sound in the deli. Not even the low rumbling of a machine. I was deaf.

I squeezed the sandwich and felt the juices trickling down in my hand. How delicious it was. I wanted to shove it in my mouth, and feel that magical taste again.

The thrum beat again, this time I identified the source of it. It was coming from inside of me. It was my heart. It pulsated inside my chest and every minute or so it thrummed so hard I could feel it echoing between the walls.

Why did the man tell me his story? Was he even a cook? He wore a long sleeve shirt that he had folded up to the elbows, long black pants and expensive looking shoes. He had three children, Gaby, Ari, and the eldest. The kids had skinny legs and ran around the yard. Why did they have a big blue doll chasing them around? Why is the mannequin blue? Why is she on a wheelchair?

My first guess must have been correct, it was a spell after all. Maybe it was their mother trapped inside that plastic body. Maybe, when the head was placed and she had a sip of water, she came back to life... But why was she blue? I think I am going mad.

No... I have gone mad.

My heart thrummed again and this time it started pulsating faster, as if I was running a marathon. The dim light coming from the outside started to fade away. The walls and the painting loomed over me. The carved flowers tedded, the painted vegetables shrunk and turned brown, and the paintings frowned.

My eyes were wide open, but my sight was black. I could hear the silence. That same silence that pierced so deep it screeches. Time slowed to an eternity for each tic. I was in that familiar void again. The void where pure energy lives. Emotions devoid of all their meanings floated in every colors in front of me.

“Am I dying?” I asked out loud to no one in particular. The colors stopped floating and turned to me. My heart pulsated in those violent thrums each making my entire body jolt.
“I'm sorry, I'm so sorry”. I cried. The colors looked at me with menacing glares. I felt the life drain out of me. The colors paled and a cold sensation started to overwhelm my body. They were like an excruciating presence of an absence.

“My God! The cook! The cook is the reaper.” I yelled. I finally got it, he was telling me of my death in riddles. He was preparing me for the pain to follow and I had seen nothing coming. How could I have been so stupid. It's like my heart knew it and it was trying to escape my body. It didn't want to die.

I wrapped my arms around my chest. Each thrum louder and stronger, cracking the walls surrounding me, cracking my chest. And now, for the first time, I was afraid. I looked straight into the abyss that was now my surrounding. Deep into the nothingness. And then, it appeared. Fear.

It was a long drape of darkness that danced alone in the far horizon. It swirled up and down in violent movements. I wanted to run and hide but I was paralyzed. It turned and saw me. It stopped and looked at me with menacing red eyes.

Before I could utter a sound, the drape cracked into motion and flew towards me. It swirled around my body. Starting at my toes, spinning around my waist, wrapping my neck, and then snapping into a tight squeeze. I gasped. I wanted to yell but my voice was muffled. So I screamed in my head.

“I'm not ready to die”, I yelled. “I don't want to die. Please don't take me.”

It's head floated an inch from mine and it squeezed my body until my mouth opened in a silent scream. All I could feel were the violent heartbeats. The figure turned into a pulsating red devil. Its eyes stayed fixated at me, looking deep into my soul. It was killing me and watching every moment of my suffering.

I never had a chance to be brave, to fight back, to say my piece. I once had dreams. I was ambitious and eager to explore the world. I wanted to learn, to grow, to teach and make a difference. I wanted to be called for help once or twice, then run over to offer my expertise. All I ever did was prepare for life, and before I could live it, it was taken. I was dying and the eyes were watching me wither away.

Now I get it. All I ever did in life, was prepare to die.

There was no need to struggle any longer. What is pain before death? Everything leads to death anyway. It was clear. Once you know it, there is nothing left to fear. I looked straight ahead, into its eyes, at the reaper, at the lord of darkness, at fear itself. And the most natural thing that came to me was to let out a smile. So... I smiled.

A hand landed on my shoulder, my heart stopped. My whole body jerked just enough for my sandwich to fall off my hand. I watched it fall. I watched it spin slowly as it unwrapped in slices of lettuce, meat, cheese, and those secret ingredients that gave it that magical taste. My eyes followed it until it fell on the greenest of grass, landing in a cheerful bounce.

I looked up and the walls were gone. The sky was clear. The sun was warm. There were trees in the distance. I could taste the moisture in the air, a river trickled not too far away. A second hand landed on my shoulder. I closed my eyes and felt each of the fingers caress me. They were thin and delicate. They were pleasant.

“You are going to be alright,” the voice said.

I turned and opened my eyes. Her hands were soft yet strong. She had golden brown hair flowing in a soft breeze that revealed her big hazel eyes. Her skin was... blue. Not just a hint of blue. It was blue like Brunnera, blue like Forget-me-not, blue like Hyacinth, blue like Morning Glory, blue like Mirabilis...
“Mirabilis aren't blue!”

You are right dear. It was blue like Love in a Mist.

My legs gave out and I was falling. I was falling back. She held out her hand grabbing my own and guided my fall. I landed on thick comfortable grass as fluff as a pillow.

She looked deep into my eyes and I was content. I returned her look and a smile grew on her lips. I didn't want to use any word to ruin the moment, so I stared at her beauty silently, smiling back.

Her fingers combed through my hair. “You don't have to worry anymore. I'm right here.” I was laying on the grass, my head resting on her lap. I looked away for a moment and I saw my coworkers by the bench, under the tree just like they had promised.

“My friends, they have waited for me.” But my voice was only a whisper. So faint, I doubt anyone had heard it. They were watching me and the blue girl like we were behind a screen. They looked emotional. Santa's little helper's held on to the beard's arm and he held her back. Their eyes were glittering.

I felt happiness. But I knew what was happening. I was dead. Stone cold dead. Not only that, but I had been murdered. But what a wonderful moment this was. If all my life had led to, was to die in the arms of this beautiful blue skinned girl, Oh then what a wonderful life it was. If the cook only knew. Death is scary on one side, but on the other? It was joyful.

Once his wife was released, she must have passed through these plains with the beautiful grass and a soft breeze. She must have found happiness the same way I do now.

I drank my fill of beauty and felt good now. I was ready to go. So, I closed my eyes and released the world. Now it was its turn to release me.

“I want to see your eyes,” she said. I only smiled. When you think you have reached apotheosis, life can surprise you with tricks you would never expect. She kissed me. My eyes opened instantly. Her lips were of a darker shade of blue, it tasted sweet like blue berries.

I closed my eyes again, I knew if I kept them closed she would kiss me again. She kissed me. This time, I refused to open them. As long as I kept them closed, she would have to kiss me. And she kissed me again.

I felt her hand rub through my chest, never knowing when she had unbuttoned my shirt. She put a hand on my heart. It was so warm. I could feel my heart starting gently, then beating with excitement like it wanted to hold out its own hand and touch her. The sun was warm on my skin. I opened my eyes and there she was smiling. It must have been the smile that had reassured the cook.

She giggled, covering her lips with the tip of her fingers.

“I know you”, I said in that faint whisper no one heard. I knew her. “I remember that giggle.” Her face was as clear as a bright blue sky and the sirens sang her name.

“Tell me everything about yourself.” she asked. “Tell me everything about your life that led to this moment. Talk to me, make a sound, say something. Anything.”

I knew the story. It was my story. A beautiful story. Not only that, I knew how to tell it in loud words that everyone could hear and understand. I had lived a whole life just so I could die. Now that I have died, I have found a whole new reason to live.

It's at that moment that I looked at the beautiful girl with brown hair, hazel eyes, and peculiar blue skin and told her everything about myself at the same time.

“Provolone!”

CHAPTER 7

Elevators

Ah, laughter. What a pleasant thing.

When I close my eyes and go to that little place in my head, I don't see colors anymore. I see laughter. And then, I am reminded of a friend. An old friend.

Was it on the ninth floor I last saw him? Or eleven? I can't tell, it feels like ages ago. I heard he had moved to a different job now, but today I am reminded of him. I am smiling. Laughing. That was precisely his strength, to make people laugh for no reason at all.

He demonstrated his powers on a group of people that always stood straight and looked sharp ahead, without so much of a blink of an eye or a sign of life. They were like statues built for the sole purpose of being a presence in the elevator. He called them figures.

Every time we took the elevator, they were occupying the whole of it. Their only real habit being an intense stillness.

When I was new, I often tried to speak to them, or make a general comment to no one in particular expecting a response. I would say something like "It is cold today" or "the days are getting shorter." Elevator talk so to speak. I even tried a polite smile followed by a saluting nod. But the only replies I ever got were grunts, a throat clearing, or most commonly, a rumbling silence.

So I challenged my friend to catch their attention. It was just a passing comment, nothing serious, more like a dare with no intent on following up.

"I dare you to lure a figure into a conversation", I said to him. His eyes jittered like they were computing a solution to a serious problem.

"You got it!" He replied and extended his hand for a handshake. We shook on it. I was not sure if it was just a joke or if he would actually do it. But I got an answer shortly after.

He did more than have a conversation with the figures. He made them laugh. He made us all laugh. I laughed so hard, yet I couldn't tell you exactly which part was funny. I can't make sense of how he did. But here it goes.

We got to the elevator from the lobby. It was already packed with all the people coming from the parking lot on the base floor.

“Going up?” I asked, not expecting any response.

Some of them did not seem too pleased to make room for us, but they were figures, figures never spoke. We got in anyway.

My friend looked at me and winked. A signal that I interpreted as the perfect audience to complete his dare. I gave an approving nod. He turned back, pressed a button on the panel then stood still. He looked confident, like he had a special plan for this very situation.

I watched.

When the elevator door closed, his plan went into motion. He snickered.

It started as a faint titter, his shoulders followed up and down, shaking in coordination. The elevator was silent if not for its faint machinery. I turned and looked at the still figures. Their eyes fixated on the reflective golden door, no sound, no motion. Like freshly carved statues.

Another chuckle escaped his lips. I turned to him. He suppressed it with a hand covering his mouth. But his shoulders kept shaking, the muffled sound was turned into a shoulder dance. I turned back to look at those still faces. No sound, no motion. But wait. The eyes. Their eyes were now moving. Imagine a statue made of marble, but the eyes are moist, veiny, and it is trying to look at the fly that landed on its shoulder.

They looked tense. They tried to stay still but he was just so distracting. I started chuckling myself. I couldn't help it. I thought he must have had an amazing joke to tell, and it must have been so funny that he could not hold himself together.

My eyes traveled between him and the figures, turning my head one hundred and eighty degrees at regular intervals. I watched him laugh and dissolve the spell that had turned them into statues. The face closer to me that had first seemed reflective and made of polished marble was now turning fleshy and soft. The lips started to twitch and twist into something that looked like a potential smile.

My friend continued to laugh with greater intensity. As if the joke in his head was becoming funnier and funnier. It was infectious. Behind me I heard whispers. I turned and saw some teeth. And there was rapid breathing. The stillness was now in motion. Somewhere in the back I heard the very first laugh, but it was immediately silenced with a hand. I saw it. Everyone saw it.

It was like an old rusty gear set into motion for the first time in a hundred years. It screeched at first before it turned the elevator into a frenzy of confused laughter. Everybody joined in. It was unnatural. Imagine statues sculpted the size and shape of grown adults that suddenly came to life. They had never learned to walk, or move with grace. It was like watching a new born flaying his hands with no particular purpose.

The girl next to me had her shoulders shaking. Her head was wobbling like the spell had dissolved her neck bones a little too much. Her laugh could be confused for a cry, it came from the throat. But that happiness in her eyes was like she had been waiting for this moment her entire life.

The tallest man in the back was braying like a donkey. Another cackled. I'm ashamed to admit, but when I laugh too much I snort like a pig.

We all laughed. The figures were now people, my friend had tears in his eyes, and the joke was still untold. The elevator kept going. He already had everybody's attention, all he had to do now was deliver the fatal blow. I laughed with great anticipation.

As suddenly as he started, he stopped. He composed himself, tightening an invisible tie and looked straight at the reflective door. His skin grew pale, his arms stiffened, and his face turned absent. He transformed into a figure.

The laughter transitioned into that awkward moment between noise and the rumbling silence. There was still some rapid breathing, I turned to them and saw a group of confused people. They turned left and right looking in every direction as if it was the first time they saw each other. Their body language felt more natural now. Hands slipped into pockets, arms were crossed, eyes explored every corner of the levitating box.

For a moment, they had found a leader. One that broke the spell and turned them into people. Now he had absorbed their sins and turned into a statue. They were in desperate need for a leader.

What happened? Why did he change his mind? I turned back to him. Through the reflection I could see his absent open eyes. I turned back to them, the motion was starting to come to a halt. All their eyes turned to me in a desperate plea. I looked back a them. Every single one of them. I knew who they were but I was afraid to admit it. They were my... I didn't want to take this responsibility.

The elevator door would open any moment now. It was over. I faced the door and composed myself. Time seems to have come to a halt, our stop was not arriving.

I closed my eyes and waited. The rumbling silence came back. My body stiffened and a moment later I felt an intense stillness freezing me over. I turned into a statue.

"Hi, my name is Clara." Her hand was already into mine. And mine in hers. It was soft as silk.

"Hi... Clara. What a beautiful name." I said. She was beautiful. She had long brown hair that curled in the end and bounced. Her eyes were hazel. Her lips were full, pink, and glowing. And her smile. Oh, I was desperately in love.

I wasted only a single second wishing we were going to the fiftieth floor so I could admire her some more. But my wish was misinterpreted, the door opened behind her almost immediately.

She stepped out. I froze. She turned to see me one last time. The door started to close. What do I tell her? Something that will make this moment worthwhile. Think. Think quickly. Oh, right! My name. What is my name?

"My name is Beric!" I said. The door was closed.

“My name is Beric. It's an unusual name. When I introduce myself, people tend to ignore the B altogether. They hear Eric. Others don't even bother knowing my name. They hear Beric, check their database, can't find it under names, so they substitute it with Barry. It was annoying at first, but then someone called me Albert. Then another, Brian. I don't even care anymore. As long as I know they are talking to me, I answer.

“But Clara? There is no mistaking it. It's clear, it's precise. It's beautiful. Just like you are...”

And then I heard a slow, stretched gasp. My eyes opened. I turned to the right and saw him. It was as if all the air had escaped his lungs, his knees coiled from under him. A sudden breath intake followed then he let out a roar of laughter.

Every one and I mean everyone burst into a roar. The shock wave shook the elevator and for a moment I was frightened. But the fear drowned in the thick air that started inside my guts, squeezing my lungs and poured out as laughter. When I turned, I saw the happy faces laugh like it was the most beautiful day of their life. Their leader was back.

I saw teeth, smiles, uvulas ululating. I saw a person sinking in the back, collapsing on his feet, which made people laugh even more. Others turned to help him never stopping to laugh.

The door behind me opened, my friend put a hand on my shoulder and we walked out. The door slowly started to close. I watched the statues that had now transformed into people interacting with one another. I watched people holding hands, helping one another. I watched the door close shut while the scene continued on its own.

I could still hear the echo of that familiar sound that bounds people into friendship. The elevator retraced its steps as it went back down and down and down.

"So... what's the joke?" I asked.

CHAPTER 8

Stories

I have never seen them as attentive as they are today. They sit side by side on the log. Their hands carrying the weight of their heads and their elbows poking at their knees. The bonfire is dancing in their big eyes, their bodies are as still as marble statues.

They listen to each word as he tells them the story. They laugh. Safia laughs with pink gums where teeth had once been. She was so sad the day her first front tooth fell. She had asked me to put it back in. Instead, I introduced her to the tooth fairy to calm her down. It worked for a while but then her other tooth felt lonely, and followed shortly after. The tooth fairy was not convincing anymore. After a good cry, she crossed her arms and vowed never to smile again. But he always makes her smile. She laughs now like the little gap between her teeth is a window to a colorful world. Isaac asked for the story of how we met. He laughs too, but he is a little more reserved. He is older now and starts to wonder if the stories are just that, stories. I look at the boy's head turning slightly toward me when he becomes suspicious.

“Did that really happen mom?”

I laugh. But his father is quick into turning him back into a believer.

They look so much alike.

My head is resting on his shoulder. My arm wrapped in his. I can feel the warmth coming out of his body. I feel the vibration of his voice when he speaks. I can hear his heartbeat, speeding up, and slowing down as he tells the story. I listen to what he says. I smile. I know how the story went. I was there. I am there.

I felt the same way when mom read us stories when we were kids. I was only a girl then, but I knew all the tales. She would open a worn-out book that I had explored a thousand times. I would follow her finger as she pointed at each word. Then she would point at the pictures and make voices for each character. I watched her lips as she spoke each word like she had been a witness in the forest when the dwarves made their way home. But then, she followed a new path the author didn't bother to write.

“Mom?” I would ask. But her fingers gently combed through my hair. Gaby's big eyes were clueless to the change. So I kept silent and listened to mom's version until the end. It was different, and my younger sister seemed to love it. I enjoyed it. It turned out to be the better story. Mom's stories were always relatable.

I wish she had met him. They would get along so well. She would have loved him, the way I have loved him from the moment I first laid eyes on him.

I had imagined the sound of his voice for a long time before I heard it. He was a quiet man.

“I saw Albert today.” A friend of mine told me once. “He was in the elevator with that guy, what's his face? They were telling jokes and making people laugh.”

“I don't believe you. And that's not even his name” I answered.

I did not believe her. My elevator rides with him were silent. He would often look my way, I would smile. It was our only interaction in an elevator too crowded for a proper introduction.

I remember the first time we talked. That day, I drove to work with dad. I made sure to tell him to make a left when we were close enough to the building. He dropped me off in front of the deli. There, no coworkers would see me and suspect we were related. I like to grow through my own merits, I didn't want anyone to think my dad was the reason I work here. Plus, he loves being at the deli more than his office.

I ran across the street, making a big scene when a car had to screech to a stop. I ran to the employees elevator with a notebook hiding my face, as if a paparazzi was stalking me.

I stood waiting, trying to catch my breath hoping no one would recognize me. I fixed my skirt. I tucked my shirt in. I noticed the space where my badge should have been. I always forget my badge. I looked up, and he materialized right next to me. He was looking at the panel where the numbers counted down. His eyes met mine. He looked just as surprised to see me. I blushed.

The elevator door opened and there was not a soul in it. Just the two of us. We both went in.

What floor? I wanted to ask, but the words came out as a whisper so faint I did not even hear myself say it. So I pressed the number eighteen. I knew we were both headed to the same floor as always. I kept my head down, too shy to face him. He was behind me, standing straight with hands in his pockets. I imagined the thoughts that would be playing in his mind at that moment.

"He should make the first move." I told myself. Despite their confidence, men are terrible at first impressions.

But what would he say to break the ice? Something romantic about the moon, the stars, or my eyes? I would love to remind him of this line for the rest of our lives, making fun of him, and telling him how ridiculous he was. But then, I would confess that I loved it. The thought of it made me giggle. We were alone, together in the elevator.

He tells the story differently. I hold on to him tighter and imagine it the way he saw it happen. I listen, and I smile. Of course it happened the way he says it happened. Yet, it changes every time he tells it.

On that day, he didn't say something I would make fun of. We were standing side by side and he was silent. What would he say? I looked at him through the reflective door, and I could see his lips moving, like they were practicing. This ride was not going to last forever.

Suddenly, the elevator jerked. Just enough to crack the thin sheet of ice that was holding us silent.

“You don't have to worry, I'm right here.”

I laughed. Does this count as a pick up line? Or is it a joke? I laughed. Not because of what he said, but because it caught me by surprise. It was the first time I was hearing his voice. I did not expect it. When I play it back in my head, it does not seem like it was funny, but I liked it.

“I'm sure I can count on you.”, I replied smiling. I meant it.

It was all it took to let him in my heart. I extended my hand and introduced myself. He held it delicately. The elevator stopped, the door opened. I exited first, our handshake still in progress. I had so much to ask, to tell, to learn. But he never moved. I felt the grip of his hand, our fingers slipped. I turned to meet his eyes. He whispered his name. The door closed too fast.

I heard, “Eric”

That's not how he tells them the story today. He adds new elements to it, something Isaac can relate to. He sprinkles the story with pretty flower names, the way Safia likes them. “Mirabilis aren’t blue.” She protests. “You are right, but it was four o’clock.” he answers. It's a positive story, but I am sad whenever I remember that day.

Everyday I took the elevator, I hoped. I hoped for another encounter. But it never happened. I searched for him in the company's directory, but there were so many Erics. I thought I heard a B sound when he said his name, so I also tried for Barry. No luck.

I even tried Berry with an E. I was hopeless. I must confess, I also tried Albert. I was desperate.

He was not too far, I could feel him. It was as if we were one step away from each other yet out of sync.

He was a ghost that dissolved into thin air every time I tried to look for him. Months went by and what I dreaded the most happened:

I forgot all about him.

When other couples ask us how we met, I smile and let him answer. He has the better story. What is a story if no one can relate to it? But when my friends ask me the same question, I tell them the way I remember it.

“My father poisoned him.”

We laugh, but it is the truth. It wasn't with poison, but it had the same effect.

When he collapsed on the ground, I felt it. I felt a sudden jolt of energy that made my feet run in his direction. I had to force them to a stop, take my shoes off, and run with my own will. I heard a tear in my skirt but I didn't care. My eyes couldn't tell it was him, he was so far away. But I knew. His colleagues were standing next to him, by the bench, under the tree, confused. They didn't know what to do. I knew what to do. I was ready. I had prepared for this.

When mom fell at home I was helpless. I sat next to her and cried. I was only a girl. If dad hadn't called the ambulance it would have been the last time I saw her alive. She had been so frail, but I thought it was going to pass. It didn't. Not long after, she was gone. I learned CPR shortly after.

I laid him down properly on the grass. I pressed my ear against his chest and listened. Only a faint hiss. When I got up, he had turned blue. But he smiled, like a man who had accepted his fate.

“No”, I told him. “No. You are going to be alright.”

He closed his eyes. I took a big breath, blocked his nose with my two fingers, and blew in his mouth. “Call 911” I yelled.

The short girl by the bench fell down in panic. She crawled back to her bag where she grabbed the phone and dialed.

I placed both my hands on his chest and pumped. When I breathed in his mouth again, his eyes were closed. His skin, as blue as a Mirabilis. “Mirabilis aren’t blue mom.”

He had given up. I hadn't. I kept pressing, giving him a breath, and pressing some more.

He opened his eyes like he was waking up from a good nap. The blue was fading away. His breath slightly hissing.

“Are you OK? Do you know where you are? What happened to you? Do you know who I am?” In the stress of it all, I didn't give him time to respond. I was quivering.

“Did you eat something bad? Please tell me what happened. I'm going to...”

He lifted a hand and placed a finger on my lips. It all stopped.

He looked away for a moment, thinking. I could hear the silence in the park, where his colleagues were standing one behind the other. The wind rustled between the grass blades and the trees whispered. The gloomy sky cleared up and the sun shone on us.

He lifted his eyes back and looked at me. He opened his mouth, and then he spoke.

He explained everything in a soft whisper. He told me his story from the day he walked into the building. He told me about his uncle who meant a great deal to him. He spoke about the silent elevator rides that consumed a good part of his day. About those people who stood still and never made any sounds. He spoke about me in the third person.

He told me about the day he was alone with her in the elevator. How beautiful she was. He struggled for a moment remembering her name. But insisted that he remembered how beautiful she was. He was frustrated now. The name was on the tip of his tongue.

“Provolone... I ate provolone.” He interrupted himself.

The sirens sang behind me and all the sudden, the ambulances were there.

I stood up and shook the paramedic by the collar. “He is allergic to cheese, and he ate a large quantity. I performed CPR and he seems to be conscious now.”

“Thank you miss, this is going to be helpful. Please step aside and we will take it from here.” the paramedic answered.

My father nods when I tell him how it happened. But as a father, he only had one important question:

“So. You have a boyfriend?”

I didn't have a boyfriend. But what else was I going to say? When the paramedics lifted him into the ambulance, they wouldn't let me get in. So I told them he was my boyfriend.

“Clara,” we all heard his calm dreamy voice coming from inside the ambulance. “What a beautiful name.” The paramedic let me come along.

He always changes the story. But it is always the same. I get mad at dad sometimes. He had no business cooking in that deli. From the fiftieth floor to... I can't believe no one recognizes him.

But I understand. I can laugh about it now. I forgive him. I... thank him. Here I am now, sitting on a log, in my husband's arms, with our two children, by the bonfire. Listening again and again, for the first time, to this ever changing story about a particular type of cheese.

The End

Afterword

A friend once told me, the worst kind of stories are those that come to you in a dream. At the time, I nodded in agreement. Not because it was evident. But because I was trying to conceal the fact that I was writing a story that came to me in a dream. It's the story you just read.

I will explain its origins, but not its meaning. In 2014, I was working in a large company in Los Angeles and I couldn't help but feel like I was a cog in a giant machine. Every three months, they would give me a raise. Every six months, they would give me a promotion. But that wasn't enough to justify my time there. Every day I felt like I was getting more and more responsibility, and not because they trusted me. It was because they had found someone who had a passion for programming and never questioned the work.

Everything that came my way was treated as a technical challenge. But little by little, that passion started to fade away, and I felt uneasy. The veil was lowered, and I could see what my code was actually doing. I was not making the world a better place. In fact, it wasn't entirely honest work. It was legal, but not honest.

Every morning, I woke up with my jaws locked in a tight squeeze. In my sleep I'd grind my teeth in a fine powder. I hated my job. I was stressed, I was frustrated, but it seemed like I was the only one. My coworkers were just fine. So I sucked it up, closed myself in an invisible cocoon, and ignored my surroundings. It was my coping mechanism.

My emotional bubble popped when I went down to the coffee shop. I stood in line waiting for my turn. I ordered a simple regular latte infused with vanilla. "And the name for the order?" the barista asked. I couldn't answer. I held the whole line when my mind drew a blank. I started laughing. I couldn't believe it. It was my name, but somehow I didn't have an answer. I didn't know what it was. The barista wrote

Vanilla latte on my cup and called for the next customer. When I went home that evening, I could only feel hate. I hated everything. I hated the managers I had to report to, I hated the work, I hated deceiving the strangers who were our customers, and I hated myself most for forgetting my very own name.

That night, I fell asleep and found myself in a peculiar restaurant. I remember the way the light shone through the window as it cascaded on the chairs, the tables, the paintings. I remember the wallpaper. I remember the meticulously carved wood decorating the lower walls. I remember the scent of moisture in the air, like I wasn't too far from a river. The dream was so vivid that I could still draw the floor plan of the kitchen to this day.

I remember the cook, how he dressed, how he spoke, his accent. He was telling me about his son. How he tried to tell him a story but the kid wouldn't listen.

There was the garden, the children, the wheelchair, and yes, even the mannequin. I remember when she stood up and held my face with both hands and told me that I was going to be alright. I held her hands reassured, and cupped them in mine. I wanted to tell her everything about myself. I wanted to tell her how stressed I was, how tired I was, how depressed I was.

She had blue skin, big hazel eyes, and I could see each of her eyelashes when they slowly fluttered like butterfly wings. I knew that if there was someone who could bring me comfort, who could end my misery, who could relax my soul, it would be her. I brought her hands to my heart and decided to tell her everything. But the only word that came out was "Provolone" and I was awake.

It was 3 am and the room was a wall of darkness. My mind was already at work, trying to erase every memory of her. I grabbed my phone and vigorously started typing. I woke up hours later, never remembering when I fell asleep. Not even remembering that I had woken up in the middle of the night. The only memory left was the one I had saved on the phone.

It was a discombobulated story but each word resuscitated the memory. I could see the restaurant again. I could see the cook, his children, the garden, the wheelchair, and... her face. It was blue and she had freckles, yet she was reassuring. If dreams are to mean something, I was not sure what this one meant. But I trusted her. I knew I was going to be alright. I quit my job.

A few years later, I stumbled upon this little document on my computer where I had saved the story. I had taken up writing, and I decided it was good source material to get started. I wrote a first draft and let a few people read it to get feedback. I was asked a question that took me by surprise. As the author I should have been able to answer it, but I was just as clueless.

"Who is telling the story?"

It seemed obvious at first since it was based on my dream and my experience at work. I thought I was the main character. Many of his experiences were mine. My name is so simple, yet no one in the English speaking world could remember it. They said Abraham, Abrahim, Ibraham, Ahab, Albert. But the narrator was not as clear cut as I thought.

I was told that in chapter 7, the previous narrator had switched places with his friend. I learned that chapter one was a dazed recollection of events that didn't necessarily occur. Chapter two is the only thing that actually happened. Three and four were the perspective of a bystander. The story itself was like a wave. It constantly changed form as you turned the pages.

You can understand my surprise. I wrote the story and that didn't even occur to me. So I asked my friend who said stories based on dreams are stupid. I asked him why he thought so. He thought for a moment, trying to remember when he had ever made such a statement. Then he answered, "Oh yes! Because the story is literally handed down to you. Someone else came up with it."

That was a shocking revelation. Here I was thinking I wrote it, so I need to retrace my steps. I went to bed, closed my eyes, and fell asleep. In my dream, a cook told me a story. I met his family, I even had a word with his daughter. Then I woke up. In this world that you and I live in, I had learned about a new story that I didn't know before going to bed. And it was given to me by someone who, for all practical purposes, doesn't exist. Then where did the story come from?

The simple answer is: I don't know. I must have dreamt it up. But there is also something else we should consider: It doesn't matter.

In my story, Mirabilis are blue because they needed to be. The cook grieved his wife's death because I had to learn to grieve too. For the rest, we have to use our own imagination.

When I read the story, it reassured me. In turn, I shared it with others to give them the same comfort. I don't know where it came from but when you read it, it is your turn to tell the story.

Author

Ibrahim Diallo is a software engineer based in Los Angeles, California. He was introduced to his first computer at the age of 5. When he turned 11, he was the unofficial IT support in the Guinean consulate in Saudi Arabia.

In 2018, he was named the first man to get sacked by a machine. His story was featured by hundreds of outlets including BBC. Ever since many of his articles have gone viral. You can find more of his stories at idiallo.com

www.ingramcontent.com/pod-product-compliance
Lightning Source LLC
LaVergne TN
LVHW010627100826
845148LV00014B/3142

9781736879900